For my godchild, Bernard

Nederlands
letterenfonds
dutch foundation
for literature

This book was published with the support of the Dutch Foundation
for Literature and the Mondriaan Fund.

First published in the UK in 2017 by Lemniscaat Ltd, Kemp House,
152 City Road, London EC1V 2NX
Distributed worldwide by Thames & Hudson,
181A High Holborn, London WC1V 7QX

ISBN 13: 978-1-78807-002-7 (Hardcover)
Printing and binding: Wilco, Amersfoort
First UK edition

www.lemniscaat.co.uk

PIET GROBLER

Hey, Frog!

Lemniscaat

One very hot day, all the animals of the savannah were playing in the water and resting in the shade.

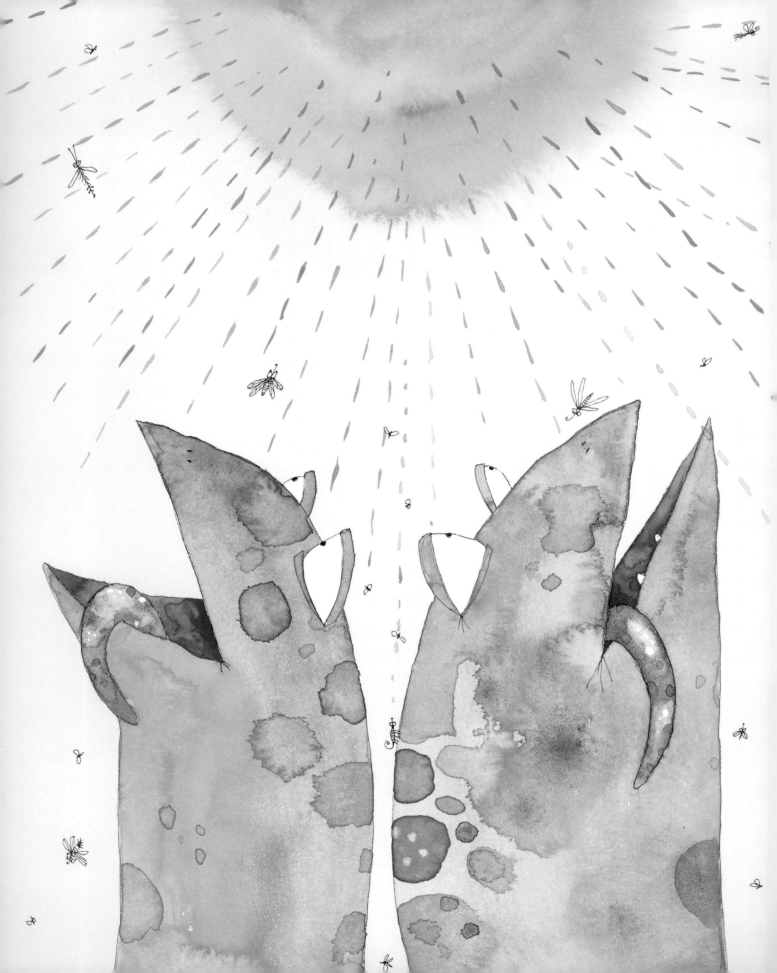

On this blazing hot day, Frog took a sip from a puddle.

"Sluuurrrp."

"Sluuuuuurrrrrrp."

He emptied the entire puddle.

He slurped up the next puddle as well,
and after that, the little brook.

He gulped up the pond and the river.
He drank up the well.
He even swallowed the big blue lake.

Soon there was not a drop of water left.

The other animals were roaring mad.
"Hey, Frog!" they shouted.
"Unzip those lips before you pop!"

Frog didn't budge.

"What can we do about Frog?" the animals wondered.

Everyone had an idea.

Lion tried to scratch the water out of Frog.

But Frog jumped away.

Chameleon tempted Frog with a fly.

But Frog was not interested.

Crocodile told Frog a tall tale about a
BIG crocodile who ate dozens of LITTLE frogs.

But Frog wasn't frightened.

Crow squawked insults at Frog.
"When he shouts back, all of you grab the
water," Crow instructed.

Crow shouted and cursed.
Frog just fell asleep.

No one's plan was working.

But the eels knew something about Frog
that no one else did.
So they jumped on Frog.
They wriggled and slithered all over him.

Frog began to twitch and shake and jerk.
Then he grinned and a little giggle slipped out.
He was ticklish all over!
Soon Frog was roaring with laughter.

And the water gushed and rushed
out of Frog's mouth, back to the puddle,
the brook, the pond, the river, the well
—and even to the big blue lake.

All the animals of the savannah were happy again. On very hot days, they played in the water and rested in the shade.

But whenever Frog looked thirsty, everyone would shout, "Hey Frog, just one sip!"